The Missing Caribou Hide

Traditional Tłı̨chǫ Stories and Legends

Wendy Stephenson and Cecilia Judas

Editing and translation by Madeline and Cecilia Judas
Illustrations by Joan Sherman

Copyright © 2022 Wendy Stephenson, Cecilia Judas & Madeline Judas

Illustrated by Joan Sherman

Cataloguing data available from Library and Archives Canada
978-0-88839-762-1 [paperback]
978-0-88839-763-8 [epub]

All rights reserved. No part of this publication may be reproduced, stored in a retrieval system or transmitted, in any form or by any means, electronic, mechanical, audio, photocopying, recording, or otherwise (except for copying permitted by Sections 107 and 108 of the U.S. Copyright Law and except for book reviews for the public press), without the prior written permission of Hancock House Publishers. Permissions and licensing contribute to the book industry by helping to support writers and publishers through the purchase of authorized editions and excerpts. Please visit www.accesscopyright.ca.

Illustrations and photographs are copyrighted by the author or the Publisher unless stated otherwise.

COVER DESIGN: J. Rade

PRODUCTION & DESIGN: J. Rade, M. Lamont

EDITOR: D. MARTENS

We acknowledge the support of the Government of Canada through the Canada Book Fund and the Canada Council for the Arts, and of the Province of British Columbia through the British Columbia Arts Council and the Book Publishing Tax Credit.

Hancock House gratefully acknowledges the Halkomelem Speaking Peoples whose unceded, shared and asserted traditional territories our offices reside upon.

Published simultaneously in Canada and the United States by

HANCOCK HOUSE PUBLISHERS LTD.

19313 Zero Avenue, Surrey, B.C. Canada V3Z 9R9

#104-4550 Birch Bay-Lynden Rd, Blaine, WA, U.S.A. 98230-9436

(800) 938-1114   Fax (800) 983-2262

www.hancockhouse.com   info@hancockhouse.com

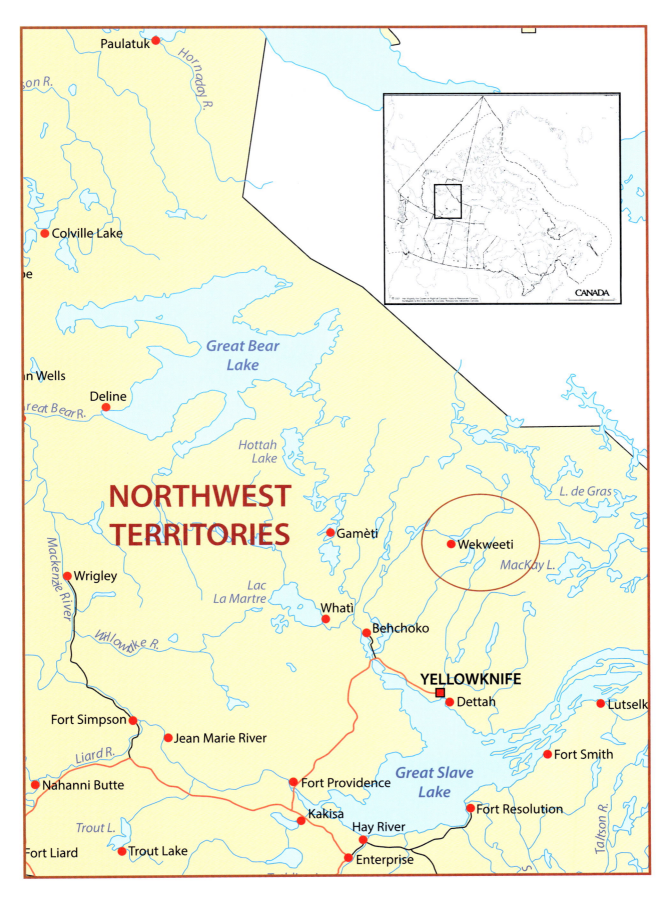

FOREWORD

It was the 70s. A group of Dechı̨ Laot'ı̨ (the 'edge of the tree line' group of Tłı̨chǫ people) led by Elders, made a decision to establish a permanent community on Wekweètì (Snare Lake). They built log cabins in the area where the ancestors frequented; living off the abundance of caribou for shelter, clothing and gear. They harvested using dog teams and most Elders still wore traditional clothing. The Indigenous community was the second closest after the Inuit to the North Pole.

The community had children of school age, as well as adults and Elders. The people of Wekweètì lobbied for a teacher, despite not having a school building. Wendy, a young teacher, took up the call and moved into a cabin heated by wood with no electricity or running water. A wall tent was set up to serve as a school.

It was not long before Wendy immersed herself into the community life and learned to speak the language to get by. The community was small; everybody looked after each other. They would have weekly prayers rotating from cabin to cabin followed by a meal together. In the winter, a hole in the ice was chopped to draw water by pails. The buildings were on a rise, a perfect natural sliding area for young people.

The villagers told stories of the past. With their voices, they told legends of people and animals that they relied on. Wendy started to make notes about her experiences living in the community. Cecilia Judas (Tłı̨chǫ, born and raised in Wekweètì and one of Wendy's students many years ago) and Wendy have turned these notes into a children's book to capture a period of time, when life was hard and simple at the same time.

John B Zoe
Tłı̨chǫ Traditional Knowledge Holder
Behchoko, NT

ACKNOWLEDGEMENTS

We would like to thank the following people for their generous help and advice with this book:

John B Zoe (for his encouragement and traditional knowledge), Judas family (for their ongoing enthusiasm, Tłįcho knowledge, translations and patience), Richard Van Camp (for his encouragement and helping us find our direction), John Lee (for his technical support and patience) and Fred Sangris (for his traditional knowledge and storytelling).

The orange December sun barely rose over the hills across the lake. It made Norma Ann squint as she sat by the window watching the children slide down the hill near her house.

She smiled as one small boy flew over a bump with a look of surprise on his face.

"**Finish making that bannock for tomorrow.**" Norma Ann turned away from the window with the sound of her granny's voice.

"**Hatsǫ gǫda łet'e net'e.**"
(Ha-tson gon-da klet-eh net-eh)

The bannock was made and now it was time for Norma Ann to go outside and saw wood for their small woodstove. As he did most days, Tatsǫ̀ with the missing feather flew down and sat beside Norma Ann on top of the woodpile.

Norma Ann smiled when she saw it and took a piece of dry meat from her pocket.

"Here you go Tatsǫ̀, I saved this for you."

"Tatsǫ̀ nàdzǫ dìyį negha wek'eadì."
(Ta-tson na-dzon di-yi
neh-gha weh-ke-a-di)

With the sound of children's laughter,
Norma Ann stopped and looked.
She watched the kids pull their
toboggans slowly up the hill and then
slide down like otters in the mud.
"Look at those kids, Tatsǫ̀. Whee!
They're having so much fun! I'd
love to slide with them one day."

Tatsǫ̀ knew Norma Ann would like
a toboggan of her own. He could
see it in the way she watched the
children. Tatsǫ̀ decided to talk to
the other animals. Maybe they
could help get a toboggan for
Norma Ann by Christmas day.

Norma Ann carried a few armfuls of wood into the house and then stopped beside her granny, **"Could I go sliding with those kids?"** she asked quietly. "You have no toboggan and we don't have enough money right now to buy one" said Granny. "Maybe Roger would let me use his sled for awhile?" Norma Ann suggested.

"Asįį chekoa gıxe zodohdzoa esanį-le?"
(ah-si che-kwa gi-hi zoe-doe-dzo-ah eh-sa-ni-leh)

"No. It's too dangerous. I need you here to help me. Christmas is in a few days and we have a lot to do" replied Granny. "Now go and feed the dogs. Uncle left some fish in the porch."

Norma Ann took the fish and walked behind the house. The sun was already setting. Another short winter day was slowly fading into a long, cold night. Norma Ann carried the fish; one for each dog and one for Nǫge with the short tail. Each day he would wait quietly behind the willow bushes for Norma Ann. She threw each dog a fish and then tossed one beside Nǫge. Before trotting away with the fish in his mouth, he stopped to look at Norma Ann as if to say thank you.

The next morning, Norma Ann took the two pieces of bannock she saved and poked her head out the door. Quietly, she made a little noise with her mouth and Nǫmba with the black spot on the tip of his tail peeked out from under the porch. Norma Ann greeted him softly and dropped a piece of bannock for him. Happily, he scurried away with it in his mouth.

She broke up the other piece of bannock and tossed it to Ìhk'aa with the grey head who was waiting outside. He hopped around gobbling up the pieces, then flew away cheerfully.

Norma Ann's Auntie lived next door. She was busy outside scraping her caribou hides to make them softer. "Norma Ann? Have you seen one of my caribou hides? I hung four hides out here yesterday and today one is missing!"

"No, Auntie, I haven't. Maybe a dog dragged it away." Norma Ann turned and walked back to her own house. She noticed her granny's hides strewn all over the porch. "My goodness! I'd better put these up on the shelf. Granny would be really upset if she saw this mess! I wonder where that long string went that tied all these hides together??" She picked them up and piled them neatly on the shelf.

"How strange! That's two things now that have gone missing" she thought to herself.

"Norma Ann! Come in now! **The floor is dirty and needs to be washed!**" called Granny.

"Detsįta dego-le t'a wek'enaıtse!"
(Deh-tsi-ta deh-go-leh t'ah weh-kay-na-ee-tsay)

As Norma Ann was about to enter the house she noticed something out of the corner of her eye. She saw Tatsǫ̀ fly by holding two sticks in his mouth. **"I wonder what Tatsǫ̀ is up to?"**

"Tatsǫ̀ga ayıı dàlea t'ı sonı."
(Ta-tson-gah a-yee da-lay-ah tee so-nee)

25

Christmas was only a few days away. All around the village people were getting ready for the special day. Mothers were sewing beautiful slippers, mukluks, gloves and jackets for their families. Fathers were busy getting their furs ready to sell. It had been a good season for trapping and this would give them extra money for Christmas. The days before Christmas were passing by quickly.

Norma Ann sat by her window sewing beads on a new pair of slippers for Granny and watching the kids on the sliding hill. "Something is funny" she thought. "This morning Nǫ̀mba didn't come by to get his piece of bannock and Įhk'aa never ate the pieces I left for him on the snow. I wonder if Tatsǫ̀ will visit me while I saw wood for Granny?"

Tatsǫ̀ never did keep Norma Ann company that day while she worked outside and Nǫgèe never hid behind the bushes to get his fish. Norma Ann went to bed that Christmas Eve feeling sad and lonely.

That night, by the light of the bright, full moon, the animals moved about quietly and carefully. Nǫgèe placed two long pieces of wood on the ground.
The ends were chewed to make them round.

Tatsǫ̀ carried some sticks and placed them across the wood. Nǫ̀mba pulled one end of the string in his mouth while Į̀hk'aa took the other end and wound the string tightly around the sticks and wood.

Next, Nǫgèe dragged the caribou hide over and slid it on top of the sticks. Tatsǫ̀ hopped on top of the hide and poked holes around the edge of the hide with his long, sharp beak.

Įhk'aa picked up the end of the piece of string once more and wove it in and out of the holes. Now the hide was tied tightly to the toboggan. With the last piece of string they made a loop in front of the toboggan. Every toboggan needs a pulling string at the front of it!

The animals rested and looked proudly at the toboggan. They were so happy to be able to give something to Norma Ann for Christmas.

It was time to pull the toboggan over to Norma Ann's house. Nǫgèe put the string in his mouth, Tatsǫ̀ and Nǫ̀mba did the same. Then they began to pull… and pull. Įhk'aa flew overhead and watched the group move slowly towards Norma Ann's house. Quietly they stopped beside Norma Ann's doorway and then scurried away.

The sun rose brightly Christmas morning as Norma Ann looked out the window.

"Merry Christmas Granny" and she gave the pretty slippers to her granny. Granny smiled and put her hand on Norma Ann's. "Masi cho Norma Ann. You did a very nice job of sewing my slippers. I am very proud of you!"

"Ehtsı̨ Taatı nezı̨ nexe weʔò."
(Eh-tsee ta-tee neh-zi neh-hey weh-oe)

As she opened the door to go outside that morning, she spotted the toboggan. It was beautiful! Not like any other toboggan in the village.

Norma Ann wondered who had made such a wonderful gift and then at once she knew. She looked behind the toboggan and saw the tracks in the snow. The tracks of Nǫ̀mba, Nǫgèe, Tatsǫ̀ and Ị̀hk'aa.

35

TŁĮCHǪ LEGENDS ABOUT ĮHK'AA (WHISKEY JACK), NǪMBA (WEASEL), TATSǪ (RAVEN) AND NǪGÈE (FOX)

Įhk'aa Steals the Moose
told by Joseph Judas (Wekweètì)

A long time ago, in the Mackenzie River area, one hunter had been following a moose for many days. Finally he caught up to the moose and was able to kill it. The hunter was very hungry from following that moose for so many days. He cut the chin off the moose and made a fire so he could eat something before he started to cut up the moose.

All of a sudden, Įhk'aa came hopping around. The hunter noticed him but didn't really pay much attention to him. He was busy cooking his little bit of meat on the fire.

Įhk'aa was hopping on the dead moose, poking here and there with his beak; eating bits of blood from the moose. The hunter looked over at Įhk'aa on the moose and got mad because he had worked so hard following the moose for so many days. And here was a little bird hopping all over the moose and pecking at it!

The hunter said, "Hey 'skinny legs'! Why are you always the first one who comes here to eat bits of meat that we hunt?" He was really mad because he was busy cooking over the fire. He wasn't paying too much attention to Įhk'aa.

Then Įhk'aa flew away. He was gone for awhile and some time later he came back. The hunter was watching him. Suddenly Įhk'aa put part of the moose head in his beak, put his wings up and flapped very hard. The whole moose head started to lift off the ground!

The hunter watched but thought to himself, "I don't think that small animal with skinny legs can take that big animal anywhere".

He kept cooking and eating and then he looked over at the moose again. Sure enough, Įhk'aa was dragging the big moose. Every time Įhk'aa flapped his wings he was moving it, and moving it and the hunter couldn't believe his eyes! The hunter got up and started running after Įhk'aa.

Just before the hunter caught up to him, Įhk'aa took that big moose and flew up above the trees with it! The hunter had no idea where Įhk'aa put the moose.

Įhk'aa had heard the hunter call him 'Skinny Legs' and heard him say, "You're the first one who comes to peck on the meat when a hunter gets an animal". When Įhk'aa heard the hunter say those things he flew back to where he came from and he told his 'boss'. Then Įhk'aa's 'boss' told him to fly back and take the moose from the hunter. In this way it would teach the hunter a lesson.

The lesson is you should never talk about animals in a bad way or tease them in any way because they all have their own boss and that's how they live. They are always listening. You never know what might happen.

Nǫmba and the Fish Guts
told by Marion and Alphonse Apples (Gamètì)

A long time ago, all the animals used to be human. One time, during the winter, people were fishing under the ice. They checked their nets each day and took the fish out of the nets. When they cleaned the fish they would roast the fish guts on the fire. Nǫmba loved to eat the roasted fish guts. Nǫmba's mother knew that and always gave the fish guts to Nǫmba first.

Nǫmba's parents went to check their net one day and came back with fish. The women and girls took the fish inside the tent and started to clean the fish. Nǫmba was hungry and wanted to eat the fish guts but felt shy to eat the fish guts in front of the other girls.

So Nǫmba sat beside her mother and started to sing, "I want to eat the fish guts. Put the guts under the spruce boughs that are on the floor of our tent. Then I can eat them later when the girls leave our tent because right now I'm shy."

Her mom was busy working on the fish and chatting to the girls. She didn't really listen to what Nǫmba was singing about so she never hid the fish guts under the spruce boughs like Nǫmba had asked. In fact, they all started eating the roasted fish guts. All except Nǫmba and then there were no fish guts left.

After the girls left the tent Nǫmba was very hungry. Since there were no fish guts left for Nǫmba all she could do was run around trying to find any bits of fish that had fallen down into the spruce boughs.

That is what Nǫmba is like today; a very fast, clever animal that goes up and down through spruce boughs, under the snow, in and out of small holes, hunting and looking for things to eat.

The Raven, the Fox and the Stolen Caribou

told by Pierre Judas (Wekweètì, 1983)

This story talks about the days of medicine power and the days when people and animals could talk to each other and change into each other. It also tells the story of respecting caribou and the importance of caribou to people.

It is believed that in the old days people had strong powers or 'medicine'. Each person had the 'medicine' to change themselves into almost any kind of animal. Life was so difficult in those days that they needed these powers in order to survive. In the following legend, the animals are really all people.

This story takes place a long time ago with a group of people living together in a small gathering of branch shelters. The people were starving. They had not seen any caribou for a long time.

During these days in which people were starving, a certain raven kept flying overhead quite happily. They people knew that the raven lived far away from them in a shelter of his own but they did not know exactly where. The little snowbirds were living with him.

Each day the people would watch the raven and wonder why he looked so healthy and happy while they themselves were starving. They decided that he must know the whereabouts of some caribou so they asked the raven about this. "No," said the raven, "Even though I am flying around all day I don't see any caribou tracks".

The people listened to the raven but they decided to follow his tracks. Once they did this, they came upon a tree. The raven had put some caribou eyeballs on a stick and left the stick in the tree. The people took the eyeballs on the stick back to a house to have a meeting about it. They wanted to make plans because they knew the raven was lying to them.

Using all their 'medicine' the people tried to decide who, among them, would be the most powerful person to go after the raven. The one with the most medicine would be the one to follow the raven's trail. Perhaps he could find out if the raven was hiding caribou!

Inside the shelter the people sat around the fire, singing and chanting to the powerful medicine man. "Go and see where the raven lives! Go and see where the raven lives!" In a deep trance, the man changed into a hawk in order to fly around in search of the raven. It was foggy however, and he could not see. "Put some ashes from the fire over my eyes" he said, "then I will be able to see more clearly". The people took some ashes and put a black line over his eyes. Soon the man could see more clearly. His 'medicine' grew very strong and he could see the direction in which the raven lived.

In the meantime, the raven had strong medicine of his own. He was able to hide many caribou, using his medicine to make a type of wall around the caribou.

Back at the house, another man decided to use his medicine and travel as a fox to try and get to the raven. He found the raven's tracks and followed them to the raven's shelter.

The raven had built a fire by his doorway so that as soon as the fox rushed inside, his tail caught fire! At the same time, the wind rushed in the door and caused the smoke from the fire to billow and fill the room. This scared the caribou, who were also gathered in the room, and they all ran out of the shelter crushing the raven as they went. All that was left of the raven was his black feathers, spread all over the ground.

This raven was special to the people. He possessed strong 'medicine' and could see into the future. The people did not want to be without him in spite of how he had tricked them. They gathered up all his feathers and used their 'medicine' to put him back together as a raven again.

The fox had not been lucky. He had scared all the caribou away. Even to this very day, some men will not wear any fox fur on their clothing when they go hunting. They believe if they did, the caribou would run away from them, just as they ran away from the fox.

Tatsǫ̀ (Raven)

Tatsǫ̀ has a character that is reflective of human beings:

- independent
- generous
- kind
- wise
- mischievous
- Tatsǫ̀ is the bird who is closest to Dene people

Nǫgèe (Fox)

Nǫgèe is described as being:

- quick
- clever
- shy
- busy
- curious

Nòmba (Weasel)

Nòmba is described as being:

- mischievous
- clever (e.g. can dance in front of a rabbit in order to distract it and catch it)
- quick
- special because it changes colour with the seasons
- good parent (it hides its young very well). As soon as the young are old enough they leave their parents to be on their own

Į̀hk'aa (Whiskey Jack or Canada Jay)

Į̀hk'aa:

- can help cure a stutter
- keeps people company in the bush
- it is good luck to feed this bird when camping
- very intelligent bird
- might be small but it is a powerful bird. Be careful what you say about this bird when you are close to it!
- it is the first bird to make a nest and lay eggs in the spring
- if children have difficulty with speaking, parents will use Į̀hk'aa to help bring language out of the child
- they are family birds (always stay together in family groups)

Information on these animals is found in Dene Kede, GNWT Curriculum

Pronunciation Guide

Tłı̨chǫ	klee-chon
Wekweètì	weh-kwey-tee
Behchokǫ̀	beh-cho-koe
Tatsǫ̀	tah-tso
Į̀hk'aa	ink-ah
Nǫ̀mba	nom-bah
Nǫgèe	no-geh

ABOUT THE AUTHORS

Wendy Stephenson

Wendy has travelled on the land and lived in various Tłı̨chǫ communities over the past forty years. She is very honoured to share a friendship with members of the Judas family who helped to write this story. Wendy has written several other children's books.

Cecilia Judas

Cecilia (Ceci) is a Tłı̨chǫ woman (daughter of Madeline and Joseph) who was raised in Wekweètì. Currently Cecilia is a teacher at the Alexis Arrowmaker school in Wekweètì. Cecilia is proud of and committed to passing on skills in her language and culture to her students. Cecilia and her spouse Clarence have three children. Cecilia was key in ensuring that Tłı̨chǫ language and stories be included in this book.

Madeline Judas

Madeline is a Tłı̨chǫ woman born in Behchokǫ̀, NT and is the daughter of Alexis and Elizabeth Arrowmaker. From the age of seven, Madeline and her family travelled the trails between Behchokǫ̀ and Wekweètì. She has lived in Wekweètì since 1963. Madeline and her husband Joseph have raised a family of nine children. They are very proud of their Tłı̨chǫ culture and way of life and have passed on their language, skills and stories to Cecilia and the other members of her family.

Joan Sherman

Joan Sherman lives in the boreal forest region of Alberta where she paints and writes about the natural world. She studied at California College of the Arts and has held drawing workshops for children and adults. Joan's paintings are in private and institutional collections. The Missing Caribou Hide is the fifth children's story she has illustrated

Other Indigenous & Children's Titles from Hancock House

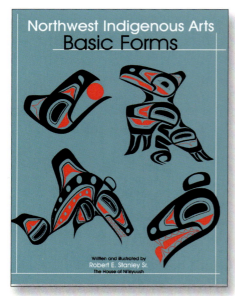
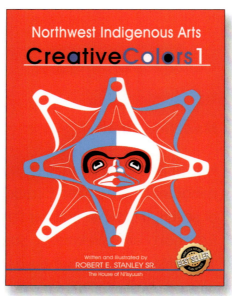
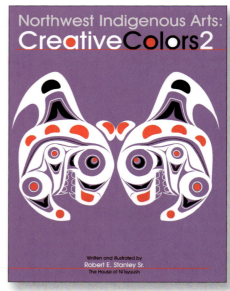

Basic Forms
Robert E. Stanley Sr.
978-0-88839-506-1
8½ x 11, sc, 64 pp

Creative Colors 1
Robert E. Stanley Sr.
978-0-88839-532-0
8½ x 11, sc, 32 pp

Creative Colors 2
Robert E. Stanley Sr.
978-0-88839-533-7
8½ x 11, sc, 32 pp

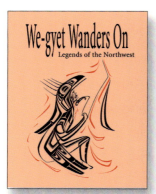
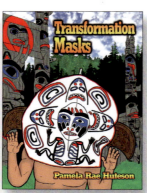
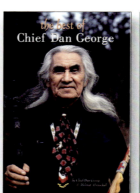
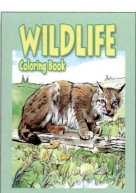
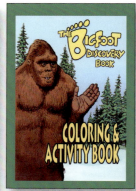

We-gyet Wanders On
Kitanmax School of
Northwest Coast Art
978-0-88839-636-5
8½ x 11, sc, 72 pp
30 illustrations

Transformation Masks
Pamela Rae Huteson
978-0-88839-635-8
8½ x 11, sc, 32 pp
30 illustrations

The Best of
Chief Dan George
978-0-88839-544-3
5½ x 8½, sc, 216 pp

Wildlife Coloring Book
Hancock House
978-0-88839-599-3
8½ x 11, sc, 32 pp

Bigfoot Coloring Book
Michael Rugg
978-0-88839-592-4
8½ x 11, sc, 32 pp

 Hancock House Publishers
19313 Zero Ave, Surrey, BC V3Z 9R9
www.hancockhouse.com
info@hancockhouse.com
1-800-938-1114